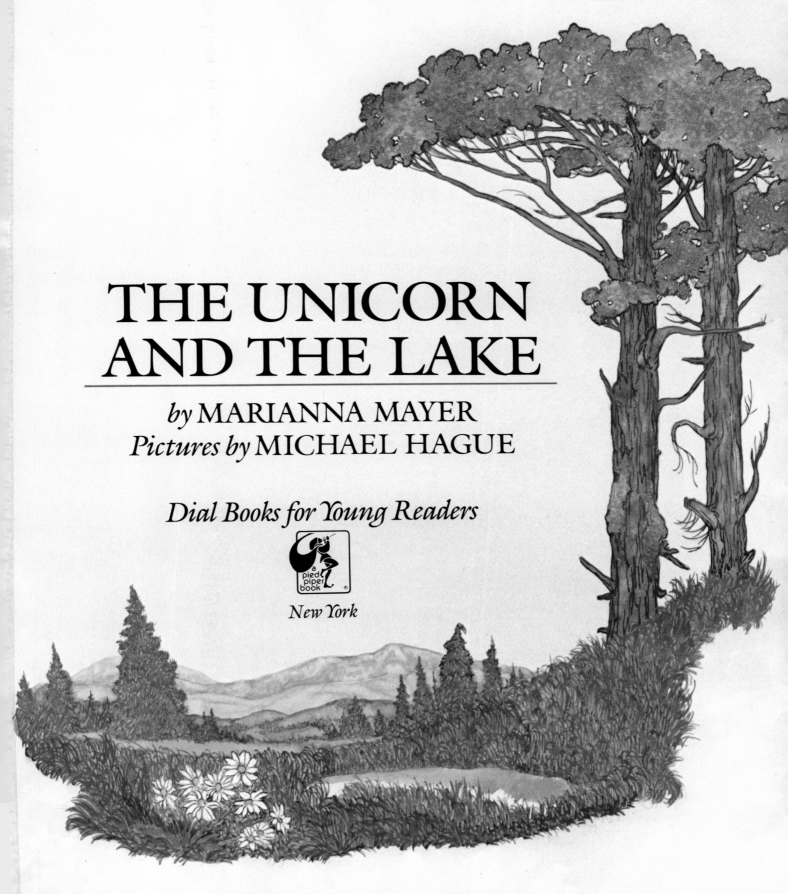

THE UNICORN AND THE LAKE

by MARIANNA MAYER
Pictures by MICHAEL HAGUE

Dial Books for Young Readers

New York

To my sister, Gabrielle Ammirati M.M.

To Nikki M.H.

Published by Dial Books for Young Readers
A Division of NAL Penguin Inc.
2 Park Avenue
New York, New York 10016

Published simultaneously in Canada
by Fitzhenry & Whiteside Limited, Toronto

Library of Congress Catalog Card Number: 81-5469
Printed in Hong Kong by South China Printing Co.
First Pied Piper Printing 1987
W
3 5 7 9 10 8 6 4 2

A Pied Piper Book is a registered trademark of
Dial Books for Young Readers,
a division of NAL Penguin Inc.,
® TM 1,163,686 and ® TM 1,054,312.

THE UNICORN AND THE LAKE
is published in a hardcover edition by
Dial Books for Young Readers.
ISBN 0-8037-0436-4

The art consists of watercolor, gouache, and ink paintings
which are color-separated and reproduced in full color.

The legend of the unicorn can be traced back to pagan times. In **400** B.C. Ctesias, a Greek writer and physician to the Persian court, reported sightings of this creature by Persian travelers to India.

The unicorn is the only fabulous beast that does not seem to have been conceived out of human fears. In even the earliest references he is fierce yet good, selfless yet solitary, but always mysteriously beautiful. He could be captured only by unfair means, and his single horn was said to neutralize poison.

The unicorn is mentioned in the Old Testament, and during the Middle Ages passages referring to him were frequently cited by theologians, encyclopedists, and storytellers. By A.D. **300** the unicorn was fully adopted by the Christian world—indeed, he had become a symbol of Christ himself.

My tale, *The Unicorn and the Lake,* is based on three specific sources. The *Physiologus,* an early Greek book of natural history, was written before A.D. **400** and elaborated upon in the centuries that followed. A later version written between the twelfth and fifteenth centuries describes the value of the unicorn's horn in absorbing poison and mentions "a great lake" where "the animals gathered…to drink." This book exists today in countless versions, most commonly known as bestiaries.

In 1389 Johannes de Hese, a priest of Utrecht, claimed to have visited the Holy Land and to have stopped at the River Marah. His observations are recorded in the *Itinerarius:*

> … And even in our times, it is said, venomous animals poison that water after the setting sun, so that the good animals cannot drink of it, but in the morning, after the sunrise, comes the unicorn and dips his horn into the stream driving the poison from it so that the good animals can drink there during the day. This have I seen myself.

My final source of material for the tale was the seven unicorn tapestries that are part of the Metropolitan Museum of Art's collection at the Cloisters. In the second of these tapestries, *The Unicorn and the Fountain,* the use of animal and plant mythology further emphasizes the borrowing of this legend. Each animal and plant depicted has an association with either the unicorn or his enemy, the serpent. The stag was believed to devour serpents, but he needed fresh drinking water to quench the poison of their venom. The theseyes flower and the common agrimony (hempe) were used against poisoning; the blue flowered sage was planted to repel snakes; the woodhaven was cultivated to keep evil away.

Today it is said that the unicorn never existed. However, it is marvelously clear that when the unicorn was first described and centuries later when the tapestries were woven, everyone believed in unicorns.

Marianna Mayer

Once long ago all animals lived in harmony. There was no strife among them, and they were able to speak together in a common language. At that time mysterious and wonderful events took place, and the noble unicorn dwelt with the other animals in the lower lands.

The unicorn was pure white, as white as mountain snow, and his ivory horn was a magnificent spiral. Men believed the unicorn was immortal. They hunted him relentlessly, for it was said that his horn possessed magical powers. At last the unicorn was forced to flee high up into the mountains to escape the hunters' arrows.

His vanishing caused magic to pass from the land. Soon all living things forgot the unicorn, and animals lost the power to speak to others unlike themselves. Thereafter, the bird spoke only to birds, the rabbit only to rabbits, the rat only to rats, and so it was throughout the animal kingdom.

During this time of forgetfulness many kinds of animals lived along the banks of a large lake. Though they could not speak together, the lake was vital to them, and they willingly shared it. Their only enemy was the serpent. He preyed upon them mercilessly, casting a shadow over their lives.

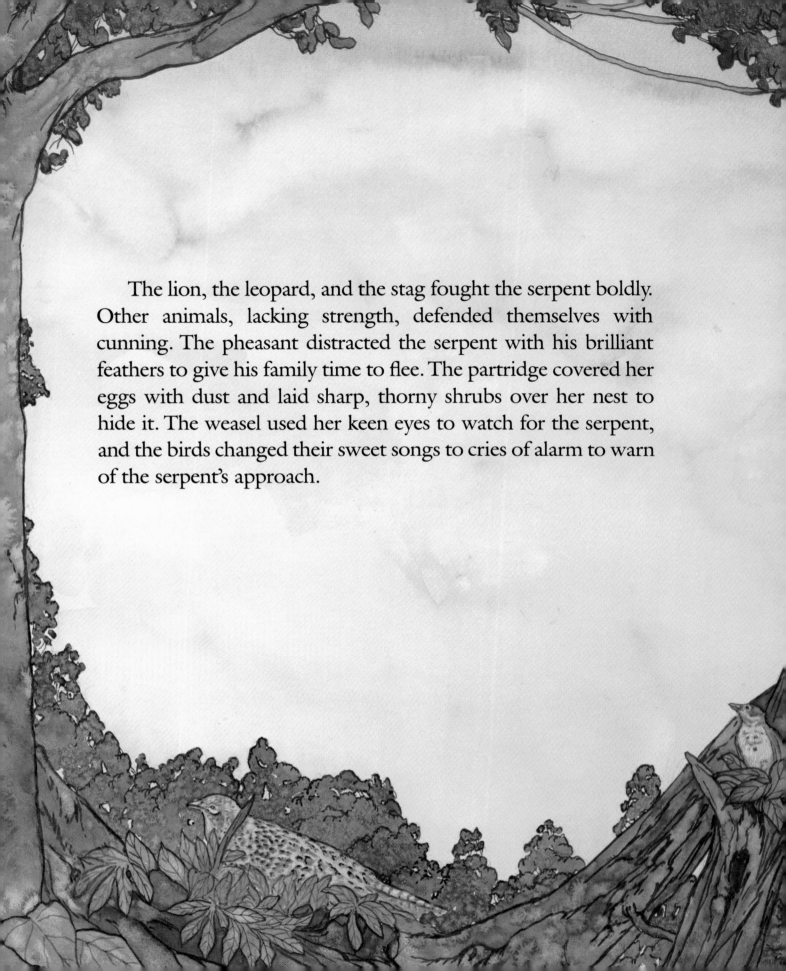

The lion, the leopard, and the stag fought the serpent boldly. Other animals, lacking strength, defended themselves with cunning. The pheasant distracted the serpent with his brilliant feathers to give his family time to flee. The partridge covered her eggs with dust and laid sharp, thorny shrubs over her nest to hide it. The weasel used her keen eyes to watch for the serpent, and the birds changed their sweet songs to cries of alarm to warn of the serpent's approach.

But in time a greater danger, a sadness, came to the forest. For months there had been no rain. Slowly the lake began to recede and the banks turned muddy. The animals struggled vainly to reach the shallow water. Many were so weak from thirst that they could no longer fight off the serpent when he attacked.

Still, no rain came. The fish were dying without water. They gasped desperately, then finally lay still and lifeless beneath the burning sun. The heron, the duck, the water rat, and other animals who fed on the water-life began to hunt in vain for other food to eat.

But the venomous serpent was glad of the others' trouble. All the better for me, he thought wickedly. Now I will not have to hunt so hard for my food.

The valley, too, began to dry without rain, and a drought fell over all the forest. The clinging green foliage that had once covered the forest floor died, and the ground cracked under the feet of the animals. Leaves from tall black walnut, beech, and oak trees turned brittle and dropped to the dusty earth.

The animals grew more desperate as each day passed. They knew that without rain to fill the lake they would surely die. Night after night the frog, who had lost his watery home, croaked mournfully for rain, but none came.

At last, leaving their natural differences aside, all the animals came together to call to the rain clouds. Ignoring the scornful serpent, they looked up at the pale moon and almost cloudless sky and called for rain to bring life back to their lake and forest.

High up in the mountains the hoary marmot, who called himself the whistler, sat at his patrol watching for enemies. As he faced the shifting wind to catch unfamiliar sounds, he heard the animals' voices and sent out a shrill cry of warning.

All the mountain animals, large and small, were alerted. Among them was one who lived in secret deep within the mountain caverns. Many years had passed since he had been seen, and his magical horn had been forgotten. He, of course, was the unicorn. Hearing the whistler's warning call, he left his den and leaped swiftly from mountaintop to mountaintop until he stood upon the highest pinnacle. Far below, the unicorn saw the animals and he understood their distress. Rearing up his powerful body, he pierced the clouds with his sharp horn. Once, twice, three times he struck the clouds. Suddenly lightning flashed and rain began to fall upon the land.

It rained that night and all the next day. Rain fell on the animals, and they rejoiced. The nooks and crannies of the mountains collected the rain and sent streams of fresh water flowing into the lake.

The serpent looked on angrily and plotted against the animals while they drank and bathed playfully in the lake. Late that night, while some slept and others were busy with their nocturnal duties, he plunged into the lake and spat his deadly venom throughout the water.

The next morning, as the nightingale sang, the animals came to the lake, but the water was dark and foul-looking, and none would dare to drink.

Again the animals cried out in anguish, and hearing them, the whistler repeated his warning. At the sound the unicorn left his cave. Far below he could see the poisoned water and the animals huddled together forlornly.

Slowly, majestically, he began to descend the mountain. As he came among them the animals at the lake stopped their shrieking and were silent. Some wept openly at his beauty; others were shy and cast down their eyes.

The serpent, coldly luminous, lay watching nearby. He alone held the ancient memory of evil, and it had given him mastery over the others. But now he felt his power ebbing away. Anger filled him, and he grew to enormous size. Suddenly he coiled and struck the unicorn from behind like a whip.

Fear gripped the animals as they watched the battle. The serpent wound himself like steel bands about the unicorn's hindlegs. A fierce war-cry came from the unicorn as he struggled to free himself. His nostrils flared, and he reared up with his forelegs thrashing. Sharp cloven hooves came crashing down upon the serpent, whose strong hold began to weaken. The unicorn was gigantic in his mighty splendor; his spirit was ruthless, and his mane flowed like windswept flames. Over and over he screamed and struck until the viper was overwhelmed and powerless.

Whirling around, the unicorn drew back and faced his enemy. Then his blue eyes caught the serpent's, and the evil one felt shame pierce his cold heart for the first time. He slithered away in fear, knowing that one of his own kind would have never spared his life.

Finally the unicorn came toward the lake, bent his proud head down, and plunged his horn into the water. Instantly the lake gleamed pure, and all the animals began to drink.

The unicorn gazed lovingly at each one. But his work was done, and he knew he could not live among them in the lower lands. Slowly he began to ascend the mountain. Where his hooves touched the ground ancient flowers bloomed once more. As he walked, a little magic passed over the animals so they were able to talk again to each other as they had once long ago. When the unicorn reached the mountaintop, the animals saw his distant silhouette etched clearly against the warming sun.

The time of forgetfulness passed. The unicorn was remembered. Springtime spread through the forest again. Everywhere leaves unfurled, fern fronds opened, and birds built nests. Masses of flowers appeared, so that the forest floor shone with color and the forest resounded with joy. Warm breezes carried the scent of rich moist soil, and dark green moss grew once more on the banks of the beautiful lake.